05/05/08

www.sugargrove.lib.il.us

RUBY in Her Own Time

For Isabelle
— J.E.

In loving memory of my
wonderful mum, Tanya
XXX
— R.H.

ISBN-13: 978-0-439-86278-3
ISBN-10: 0-439-86278-7

Text copyright © 2004 by Jonathan Emmett. Illustrations copyright © 2004 by Rebecca Harry. All rights reserved.
Published by Scholastic Inc., by arrangement with Macmillan Children's Books, a division of Macmillan Publishers Limited, London.
SCHOLASTIC and associated logos are trademarks and/or registered trademarks of Scholastic Inc.

12 11 10 9 8 7 6 5 4 3 2   7 8 9 10 11 12/0

Printed in the U.S.A.   40
First Bookshelf edition, February 2007

RUBY in Her Own Time

Written by
Jonathan Emmett

Illustrated by
Rebecca Harry

SCHOLASTIC INC.

New York   Toronto   London   Auckland   Sydney
Mexico City   New Delhi   Hong Kong   Buenos Aires

Once upon a time
upon a nest
beside a lake,
there lived two ducks —

a mother duck
and
a father duck.

There were five eggs in
the nest. Mother Duck sat
upon the nest,

all day...

and all night...

through howling wind...

and driving rain,
looking after
the eggs —
ALL five of them.

Then, one bright morning,
the eggs began to hatch.

One

two

three

four

little beaks poked out
into the sunlight.

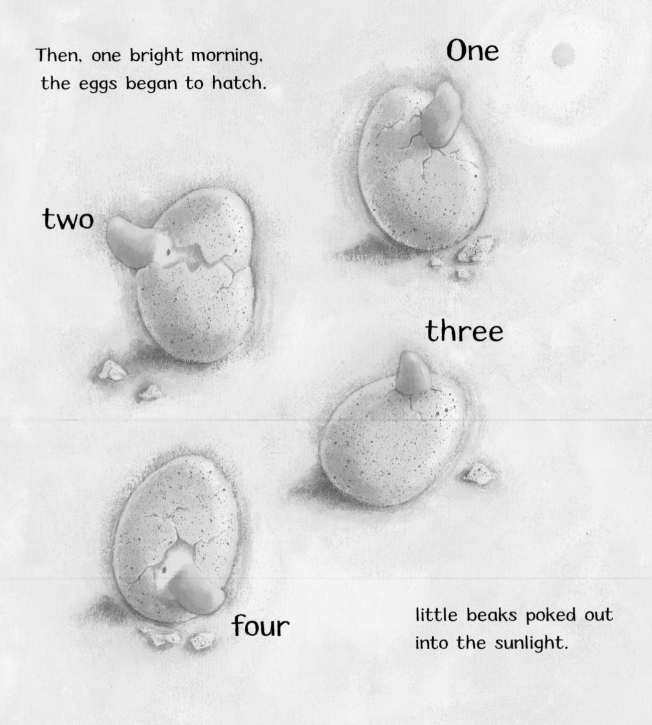

One

two

three

four

little ducklings shook
their feathers in
the breeze.

"We'll call them
Rufus, Rory, Rosie, and
Rebecca," said Father Duck.
And Mother Duck agreed.

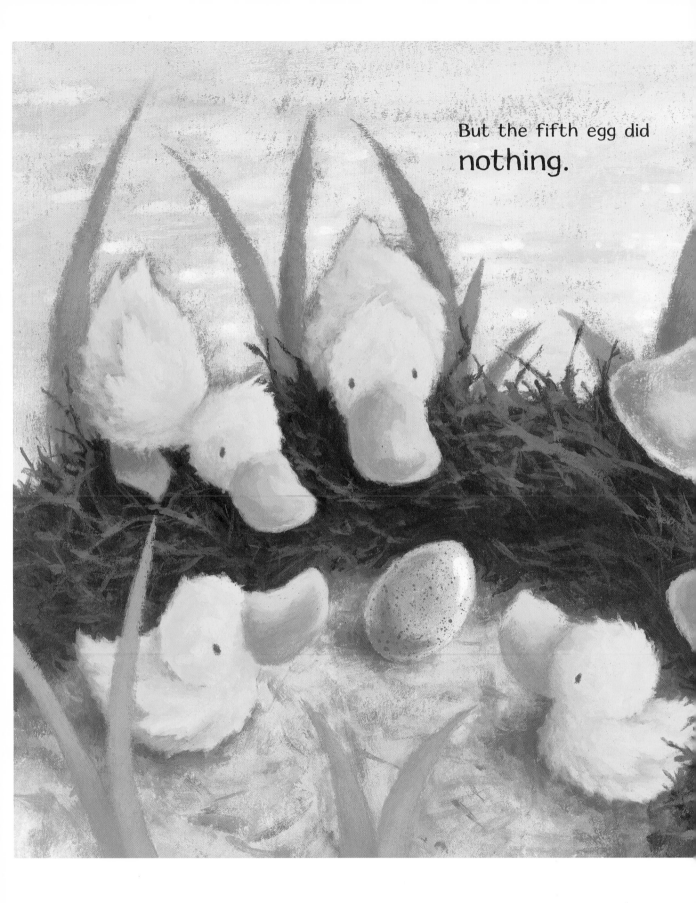

But the fifth egg did
nothing.

"Will it **ever** hatch?"
said Father Duck.

"It will," said
Mother Duck,
"in its own time."

And —
sure enough —
it did.

"She's very small,"
said Father Duck.
"What shall we call her?"

"We'll call her Ruby,"
said Mother Duck,
"because she's small
and precious."

Rufus, Rory, Rosie, and Rebecca
ate whatever they were given.

They ate anything and
everything.

But Ruby ate
nothing.

"Will she **ever** eat?"
said Father Duck.

"She will," said Mother Duck,
"in her own time."

And —
sure enough —
she did.

Rufus, Rory, Rosie, and Rebecca
swam off whenever they were able.

They swam anywhere
and **everywhere.**
But Ruby swam **nowhere.**

"Will she **ever** swim?"
said Father Duck.
"She will," said Mother Duck,
"in her own time."

And —
sure enough —
she did.

Rufus, Rory, Rosie, and Rebecca
grew **bigger.**

And Ruby grew **bigger** too. Her feathers grew out, and her wings grew broad and beautiful.

And when Rufus, Rory, Rosie, and Rebecca began to fly...

...Ruby flew too!

Rufus, Rory, Rosie,
and Rebecca flew far
and wide. They flew out
across the water.
They flew up among
the trees.

But Ruby flew farther and wider.
She flew out **beyond** the water.

She flew up **above** the trees.
She flew anywhere and **everywhere**.

She stretched out her
beautiful wings...

and soared **high**
among the clouds.

Mother Duck and Father Duck
watched Ruby flying off into the distance.

"Will she ever come back?"
said Mother Duck.
"She will," said Father Duck,
"in her own time."

And –
sure enough –
SHE DID.